For friends, near and far,
you know who you are ~ R.A.

For Han x ~ F.I.

tiger tales
5 River Road, Suite 128, Wilton, CT 06897
Published in the United States 2022
Originally published in Great Britain 2020
by Little Tiger Press Ltd.
Text by Rosie Adams
Text copyright © 2020 Little Tiger Press Ltd.
Illustrations copyright © 2020 Frances Ives
ISBN-13: 978-1-68010-277-2
ISBN-10: 1-68010-277-X
Printed in China
LT/2800/0192/0122
2 4 6 8 10 9 7 5 3 1

www.tigertalesbooks.com

The WORLD ~is a~ FAMILY

by Rosie Adams   Illustrated by Frances Ives

tiger tales

We gaze at the sunrise together
and wonder at all that we see.
There's a whole world for us to discover.
Let's explore it! Come on, follow me....

The world is a family—
we are all one,
growing together
under the sun.

High in the sun-dappled treetops,
the branches all rustle and sway.
Squirrels are scrambling and chasing.
It's good to have fun and to play!

The world is a family—
we are all one,
playing together
under the sun.

At times when our lives are so busy,
we just need to stop for a while
and make time for stillness and silence,
relax, and recover our smile.

The world is a family—
we are all one,
resting together
under the sun.

The sky hums with wings gently beating.
Songs float sweet and clear on the air.
We're free, flying high and exploring,
with wonders to see everywhere.

The world is a family—
we are all one,
exploring together
under the sun.

In the calm and the cool of the forest,
cubs search for ripe berries to eat.
They share the treasures between them.
Their friendship makes life taste so sweet.

The world is a family—
we are all one,
sharing together
under the sun.

Being part of a family is special.
It means that we're never alone.
We all have our place in the picture,
and the best place of all is our home.

The world is a family—
we are all one,
living together
under the sun.

The stars in the sky twinkle brightly.
The moon's shining high up above.
We're so lucky to be here together
in this beautiful world that we love.

The world is a family—
we are all one,
united together
under stars, moon, and sun.